GUINEA PIGS ONLINE

FURRY TOWERS

JENNIFER GRAY & AMANDA SWIFT

ILLUSTRATIONS BY
SARAH HORNE

Quercus

First published in Great Britain in 2012 by

Quercus
55 Baker Street
7th Floor
South Block
London W1U 8EW

A CIP catalogue reference for this book is available
from the British Library.

ISBN 978 1 78087 267 4

1 3 5 7 9 10 8 6 4 2

Printed and bound in Great Britain by Clays Ltd, St Ives plc.

By Jennifer Gray and Amanda Swift

GUINEA PIGS ONLINE

GUINEA PIGS ONLINE: FURRY TOWERS

For Richard
J.G.

For Robbie, Katya, Ysanne, Ezra and Joe
A.S.

For Sharon and her fluffy friends at Endsleigh
S.H.

contents

1
pamper your pet

'Oh dear,' said Coco the guinea pig, in her delicate, posh voice. (As you probably know, guinea pigs can make lots of different noises, but talking is something they only do when humans aren't around.)

Coco got no response from her

friend Fuzzy, so she tried again. 'Oh dear, oh dear,' she sighed a little louder.

Still no response! Honestly, Fuzzy could be so annoying sometimes.

'Oh dear, oh dear, oh dear, OH DEAR!' she said, and then gave a sigh so huge she nearly fell out of the hutch, where she was having a late-night read of the local newspaper.

'I can hear you,' said Fuzzy as he danced on the laptop keyboard, which Ben had left open. Ben was Fuzzy's owner, and he was rather forgetful, which was ideal for Fuzzy because it

meant he could do a little late-night surfing on the Net.

'Then why don't you ask me what's wrong?' said Coco crossly.

'Because I already blinking well know,' said Fuzzy, who was not posh at all. 'You're worried about being stolen.'

'Well, aren't *you*?' asked Coco, looking anxiously out of the

French windows into the dark night. She wished Henrietta, who was her owner, had bought some curtains for them, but Henrietta, like her husband Ben, was also rather forgetful. Sometimes she forgot to brush her hair, and sometimes he forgot to wear socks, and both of them had forgotten to have children, but it didn't really matter, because Fuzzy and Coco were just as adorable as children, with the added attraction of having lovely soft fur. 'What if someone comes and steals us tonight?' asked Coco in a worried voice. 'Like those other guinea pigs.'

'They won't,' said Fuzzy, sliding his bottom along the mouse in order to change websites. 'The doors are locked. Ben and Henrietta are asleep upstairs. If anyone broke in, they'd hear and come and save us.'

'But what if . . .' Coco paused dramatically and glanced at Fuzzy to make sure he was listening. Sure enough, he had stopped tapping on the mouse and was lying still, ears back. She continued in a little, squeaky voice: '. . . they come while Ben and Henrietta are away?'

This is what Coco had been

sighing about all along. Ben and
Henrietta were due to go on holiday
in only two days' time. They were
going to save seals down on the coast,
which wouldn't be a holiday for most
people. What's more, Henrietta was
a vet, and Ben worked for an animal
rescue centre, so it really was a bit like
their work. But then again, they loved
all animals, and most people try to do
what they love on holiday, and for
Ben and Henrietta that was rescuing
seals.

'We'll just have to run away and
hide somewhere where they can't

get us,' said Fuzzy, trying to sound tougher than he felt.

'But the Sheltie who was taken was really fast! He won the Rodent Race at his owner's school!' exclaimed Coco, tapping the photo of a handsome black and white long-haired guinea pig in the newspaper. 'And he got stolen. He was a rare breed too, like some of the others. So in total that's fifty-five guinea pigs stolen in the Strawberry Park area since Christmas. I dread to think why they're being taken. I hope it isn't Scarlet Cleaver up to her tricks again.'

Scarlet Cleaver was a famous chef who had stolen guinea pigs because she wanted to cook them. She had even stolen Fuzzy. Luckily Coco had been able to rescue all the guinea pigs, with a little help from her new guinea-pig friend Eduardo and Her Majesty the Queen.

'Scarlet Cleaver's still in prison,' Fuzzy reminded Coco. 'And anyway,' he said, glancing at the newspaper, 'that doesn't look much like Scarlet Cleaver, unless she's grown a beard and started wearing a hat.'

A grainy photograph of the suspect stared back at them from the page. Coco shivered. 'Imagine meeting him on a dark night!' she squealed. 'I mean, what if . . . ?'

'What about this?' Fuzzy interrupted. He was staring at the

computer screen. Coco came and sat next to him on the mouse.

'"Come to Furry Towers",' Fuzzy read out loud, '"the Ultimate Five-Star Guinea-Pig Hotel".'

'Guinea-pig hotel?' repeated Coco. 'Now you're being silly, Fuzzy.

There's no such thing as a guinea-pig hotel.'

'Yes, there is, Coco. Look!'

Coco reluctantly looked up at the screen. She wasn't very keen on computers. She much preferred newspapers, and chatting with her guinea-pig friends, like Banoffee, who lived next door.

'"Let us pamper your guinea pig!"' she read. '"Furry Towers offers the ultimate cavy experience – from our luxury accommodation to our state-of-the-art beauty spa. Your pet will have sweet dreams on our handpicked hay beds. Meals are served in the deluxe hutches or out in the spacious runs and consist of organic vegetables delicately shredded or diced. Let your pet exercise in our fully equipped gym, an exact model of the Olympic training facility, and relax afterwards in the spa, where he or she can enjoy an aromatherapy bubble bath followed by a blueberry-and-vanilla facial."'

'Oh, Fuzzy,' Coco sighed, only this time it wasn't a worried sigh – it was a happy sigh.

'You like it, don't you?' He looked

at her lovingly, because they did love each other; they just weren't *in love* like Ben and Henrietta.

Coco nodded her head. 'I would want to go there even if there wasn't any guinea-pig-napping going on. It sounds the most wonderful place in the world. I wish the holiday started tomorrow . . .' Then she looked worried again. 'But how will we get Ben and Henrietta to take us there? They might not even know about it.'

'Easy,' said Fuzzy, tapping a couple of keys on the computer. 'We just leave this page open for Ben to read.'

'I see,' said Coco, although she didn't really see how a screen could have a page. She wasn't going to admit that to Fuzzy though.

Next morning, the first thing Ben did when he came down to the kitchen was to check on the guinea pigs, because he too had heard about the guinea-pig-nappings and wanted to make sure that Fuzzy and Coco were still safe in their hutch. Neither Ben nor Henrietta had any idea that the guinea pigs were so clever they could let themselves out when the humans weren't around. Happy to see them sleeping safely in the soft hay, he went over to the computer to look at the day's news.

To his surprise, it wasn't showing its usual home page. It was open on a website he hadn't seen or heard of before:

Come to Furry Towers, the Ultimate

Five-Star Guinea-Pig Hotel!

What a good idea, he thought, because he and Henrietta had been talking about the guinea-pig-nappings only the day before, and had agreed that it was a worry to leave Fuzzy and Coco with the little girl down the road only coming in once a day to feed them. With no one living in the house, they would be easier to steal. 'Henrietta must have found the site after I went to bed,' he said aloud, 'and left it open for me to see.'

When Henrietta got up, she thought the same as Ben did. Ben

must have found the website while she
was having her bath,
and had left it open
for her to see.

Over breakfast they decided to send
their precious guinea pigs to the hotel.

'You are clever, darling,' Henrietta
said.

'So are you, darling,' Ben said.

'It's the perfect solution – to send them to a hotel.'

'Yes, perfect.'

While Ben gave the guinea pigs their morning stroke, Henrietta picked up the telephone.

'Hello, is that Furry Towers?'

Coco and Fuzzy listened eagerly.

'Do you have space for two guinea pigs for a week from Wednesday?'

The two guinea pigs held their breath.

'You do? That's great!'

Coco and Fuzzy started squeaking with delight.

Ben looked at them fondly. 'If I didn't know better, I'd say you two already knew you were going on holiday!' he laughed.

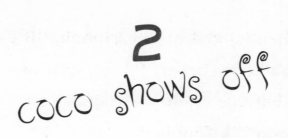

2
coco shows off

As soon as Ben and Henrietta left
for work, Fuzzy and Coco let
themselves out of the hutch and
scrambled through the old cat flap
in the back door, which they used to
get in and out of the garden. They
couldn't wait to tell Eduardo and

Banoffee the exciting news about their holiday!

'Cooee,' Coco called. 'It is one!' (Coco had a habit of saying 'one' instead of 'me' or 'I', because when she was younger she had lived with the Queen and she thought it made her sound grand.)

'It's two actually!' Fuzzy shouted, chasing after her.

A few minutes later the four guinea pigs had gathered by the mouldy wooden gate at the end of the garden, which led into the copse where Eduardo lived.

'A hotel!' Banoffee gasped. 'Just for guinea pigs?'

Fuzzy nodded. 'The food looks fantastic!' he said, sitting back and patting his round tummy. 'I'm hoping for avocados!' Fuzzy loved his food –

the more the better, especially if it was avocados.

Coco frowned at him. 'They're full of fat, you know.'

'But I'll be going to the gym, so it'll be OK,' he said confidently.

'I'm going to spend lots of time in the spa!' Coco boasted.

'Oooh!' squealed Banoffee. 'You lucky things!' (Banoffee had a lot of children so she didn't get to relax much.) 'Are you going to have your nails painted, Coco?' she asked eagerly.

'Oh yes! And my whiskers curled

and my hair styled every day!' Coco told her. 'And a massage and a blueberry-and-vanilla facial and—'

But Coco didn't manage to finish telling Banoffee all about the other wonderful things she was going to have done at the guinea-pig hotel because she was rudely interrupted by a loud snort.

'Does one need a tissue, Eduardo?' Coco asked coldly.

'No, señorita!' Eduardo chuckled. 'I don't have a cold – I am snorting with laughter.'

'What's so funny?' Fuzzy asked, although he thought he knew. Coco had lovely caramel fur with pretty little twists called rosettes. The idea of her being covered in squashed blueberries made him want to giggle too.

'You pets crack me up!' Eduardo doubled over with laughter. 'A guinea-pig hotel! *Caramba!* You're crazy!'

Eduardo was a handsome silver-and-black guinea pig who came from Peru. He had travelled all the way to England by boat to help free

the guinea pigs of the world, only
to find they preferred to stay with
their owners! At first he was quite
disappointed that Strawberry Park
seemed so boring, but he liked living
in the copse and writing songs and
annoying the bad fox called Renard
who was always trying to eat the
other animals, so he stayed on. And
he was glad he did. Eduardo had
already had one exciting adventure
with Fuzzy and Coco – catching the
horrible Scarlet Cleaver. In fact he'd
been hoping when he heard Coco call
for him that morning that she had

come to tell him about another one.
But he couldn't think of anything less
exciting or adventurous than staying
in a guinea-pig hotel, which is partly
why he wasn't being very nice. The
other part was because he suddenly
realized he couldn't go to the hotel
even if he wanted to, because he had
no one to book him in or pay for him.

'You'd never get a freedom fighter
like me into one of those places,' he
boasted loudly.

Coco frowned. She had wanted
Eduardo to be impressed. 'Why not?'
she asked crossly.

'Because hotels are for softies, not for tough guys like me!' Eduardo threw his satchel over his shoulder and started to walk away.

'Softies?' Coco shouted crossly. 'Is that what you call us behind our bottoms?'

'Sure. That's what you are, right?'

Eduardo turned round to give her a wave. 'Have fun with your facial!' he said, forcing himself to grin even though he didn't feel like it. He disappeared through the hole in the gate.

'Nobody asked you to come anyway, Eduardo,' Coco yelled after him, forgetting she was posh. 'We all know you prefer rolling around in mud and . . . and —' she tried to think of something hurtful to say — 'writing terrible songs, so have fun yourself with all that while we're away!'

Eduardo's nose poked back through the gate. He gasped. 'Are you saying my songs are not good, señorita?'

'They're rubbish!' Coco yelled.

'Then I will never write another one.' The nose disappeared.

'Coco!' Fuzzy was shocked by the argument. 'Eduardo was just kidding. He doesn't really think we're softies.' He looked thoughtfully at the hole in the gate. 'And anyway, don't you think he might be a little jealous that we can go to a hotel and he can't? You didn't have to be so mean about his songs.'

'He wasn't kidding!' It was Coco's turn to snort (delicately of course), but this time she did need a tissue, because she was about to cry, not laugh. She hated being made fun of, especially by Eduardo, whom she secretly admired. And now she felt guilty as well, because what Fuzzy said might be true. Eduardo didn't have an owner. He couldn't go to the hotel even if he wanted to. 'Oh . . . oh . . . oh . . .' She burst into tears.

'I think you need a holiday!' Fuzzy said kindly.

'I agree, Coco.' Banoffee nodded,

rubbing her
shoulders.
'Don't worry,
dear. You'll
forget all
about it
when you
get into that
nice warm
jacuzzi.'

3
mouldy towers

It turned out Banoffee was right – Coco did forget all about her argument with Eduardo – but for the wrong reasons. By the time the guinea pigs arrived at Furry Towers two days later, Coco was in such a tizzy she barely remembered anything.

35

The problem was that the guinea pigs had never been to stay away from home since they had been living at number 7, Middleton Crescent, and Ben and Henrietta were very anxious. First of all there was a big fuss about the guinea pigs' travel arrangements. Ben said that the hutch was too big to move, so Henrietta spent ages looking for a cardboard box that would fit in the car. Then, when she finally found one by throwing everything out of the garage, Ben spent ages painting the outside of the box to make it look nice and cutting breathing holes so that the guinea pigs wouldn't suffocate. Then Henrietta, who was a vet after all, started to worry that they would suffocate because of the smell of paint. So in the end she and Ben rushed off to the pet shop and bought a special guinea-pig carrier.

After that there was the business of getting all their things ready. Fuzzy didn't need anything except a bottle of water for the journey, but Coco needed all sorts of stuff, like a comb and some bows and a pair of nail clippers, which Henrietta had put in a safe place and couldn't find.

Finally they all got in the car.
Henrietta started the engine and set off.

'Which way?' she said.

'I don't know,' said Ben.

'I thought you checked the
directions.'

'I didn't have time. I thought you
checked the directions.'

'We haven't got time to go back now,' said Henrietta.

'It can't be far,' agreed Ben.

An hour later, when they were still driving round and poor Fuzzy and Coco (who had both eaten too much grass) felt quite sick, they stopped and asked a policeman if he knew where Furry Towers was.

'It's just up the road,' he said, helpfully pointing.

A moment later the car pulled over again.

'Thank goodness. Here we are at last!' Henrietta said.

The guinea pigs sighed with relief when they felt the car come to a halt. There was a clunk as the car door opened. Then they felt their carrier being slid along the back seat and lifted into the fresh air.

Coco and Fuzzy wriggled out from under the straw where they had been hiding and pressed their faces against the narrow air holes.

Ahead of them, up a little path flanked by pretty rose bushes, they saw a small house that looked a bit like theirs, except this one was covered in lovely blue flowers. It had

a beautiful front garden and a painted
sign saying 'Furry Towers'.

'Rose bushes!' Coco said dreamily,
beginning to feel better. 'Oh, Fuzzy,
isn't it lovely?'

'Look at the lawn!' Fuzzy's eyes grew round. The grass was lush and green and tasty-looking. 'Imagine eating that!'

'Hello, hello, hello!' A man came out of the house and hurried down the path towards them. 'How lovely to see you!' He smiled at Ben and Henrietta. 'It's Fuzzy, isn't it?' he said, nodding towards the pet carrier. 'And

Coco?' He put out his hand to take it. 'I'm Nigel.'

For one tiny moment Coco noticed that the man had forgotten to put ladies first, which she knew was VERY BAD MANNERS, but then she got distracted by the thought of the jacuzzi and the fact that Nigel was very good-looking for a human.

'Oh, er, OK, er . . . Nigel . . . here you are.' Ben handed him the carrier carefully. 'You will take care of them, won't you?' he said, bursting into tears. 'Only they've never been away from home before.'

Nigel smiled. 'Of course we will!' he said smoothly. 'At Furry Towers I guarantee we care for our little guests' every need.'

'Jolly good,' said Henrietta, who was much more practical than her husband.

She reached into her handbag and produced a handkerchief, which she gave to Ben, and several pieces of paper stapled together. 'This is a list of all their requirements,' she explained. 'It tells you when they need to be fed, what they like to eat, how many times to change their straw and which lullaby to sing them when they go to bed.'

'Marvellous,' said Nigel, taking the pieces of paper in his free hand.

'Should we come in and settle them down?' Ben sobbed.

'No need for that,' Nigel said quickly. 'I imagine you want to be off. You're quite a bit later than I expected.'

'Nigel's right,' Henrietta said firmly, taking Ben's arm and steering him down the path back to the car. 'We are very late indeed, and we

have sick seals to
rescue. Come on,
Ben. Coco
and Fuzzy
will be fine.'

The guinea
pigs heard them
get back into the
car and drive off.
They felt a little sad,
but the truth was they didn't really
mind too much because they were
so excited to be at the hotel. They
looked up at Nigel expectantly.

Nigel raised the carrier towards his

46

face and squinted back at them. His smile faded. 'Huh, stuff this,' he said sourly.

To Fuzzy and Coco's amazement he dropped Henrietta's list on the ground and kicked it under a pile of leaves.

Nigel scowled at them for a few seconds more. 'You're not what I'm looking for,' he snapped, swinging the cage backwards and forwards so that the guinea pigs felt sick again. 'You're just ordinary guinea pigs.' He pulled a face. 'I'll put you in the garden with the others.'

He marched towards the house and into the hall. 'Lullabies, indeed!' the guinea pigs heard him snarl angrily. 'For these two!' He laughed nastily. 'I don't think so!'

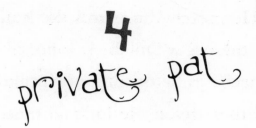

4
private pat

As Nigel hurried through the hall Coco managed to notice the rather attractive guinea-pig design on the wallpaper, featuring all kinds of exotic breeds interspersed with cabbages and carrots. She remembered it from the photos on the hotel's website. She

made a mental note to look it up on
the Internet when she got home and
leave the page open for Henrietta and
Ben to notice it, buy it and then put it
up. She was getting the hang of
this Internet business, she thought
proudly.

Nigel took them through a door
in the hall and into a conservatory. It
wasn't like the conservatory at home,
with its sofa and computers; this one
had a long counter and a basin and
lots of bottles of what looked like
beauty products. Perhaps this was
where the spa was? Coco couldn't

smell blueberry
or vanilla, but
she did see
a beautiful
guinea pig
with long white
hair lying on
what looked like a velvet cushion.

'Hello – I don't think we've met.
My name is . . .' Coco started to
say, but she didn't have time to finish
because Nigel had got as far as the
door to the garden, which he yanked
open. The guinea pigs felt a rush of
fresh air. Nigel walked out into the

garden and plonked the pet carrier on the ground.

'Where are we going?' Coco cried. 'The spa's back there!'

'Perhaps we're going to the spacious run first,' suggested Fuzzy, 'to meet the other guests.'

He looked out through the holes. There was no sign of a spacious run; all he could see was fading flowers and dead grass and a black leafless tree

that loomed over the garden like a witch over her cauldron.

Suddenly Nigel lifted the pet carrier, tipped it up, opened the door and let the guinea pigs fall any old how into what seemed like a dark wooden toilet. (It wasn't a toilet – it was a hutch, but it smelt like a toilet.)

'Home sweet home for the next week!' called Nigel as he locked the hutch door, and then he left.

'Home sweet home for the next week?' squealed Coco. 'He's got to be kidding, right?'

Fuzzy looked embarrassed. He had
a horrible feeling Nigel wasn't kidding
at all.

'Right?' Coco demanded.

'Er . . .' Fuzzy couldn't think of
anything to say.

'You idiot!' Coco snapped. 'You
believed everything it said on the
computer!'

'OK, so maybe it wasn't all true.'

'The bit about the perfumed hutch
certainly wasn't,' said Coco, holding
her nose. 'Unless they've invented
a new perfume called Eau de Wee-
Wee.'

'Let's see if there's anything to eat,' said Fuzzy, twitching his nose in search of food. He didn't want to make Coco any crosser by telling her he'd already picked up the smell of rotten cabbage. 'Ah, here we are,' he said, trying to sound cheerful as he trotted over to the food bowl in the corner.

'Are you sure that isn't the

compost bin?' said Coco. 'It certainly stinks like the one at home.' As she spoke Coco felt a pang of sadness in her heart. She was missing Ben and Henrietta; she was missing home; she was even missing the smelly compost bin. Fuzzy picked up on her sadness even though she was silent. He looked around the hutch in the hope of finding something to cheer her up, but there was nothing there except a huge pile of hay in the corner.

'At least there's lots of hay to sleep on,' he said, patting the pile. 'It feels quite . . .' He was going to say 'soft'. But it wasn't soft. There was something hard underneath. He moved the hay aside. 'What the . . . ?' he mumbled. 'There's something under here, Coco!'

'Is it the bubble bath?' asked Coco wistfully, moving towards him.

'No, it's –' he cleared more hay – 'it's made of metal. It's green . . .' He cleared a little more.

'A hairbrush?' suggested Coco.

'No, it's much bigger than that.' Fuzzy was moving great clumps of hay now, as quickly as he could. 'It's a vehicle, Coco, a military vehicle. I think it's a . . . tank!' One side of the tank was visible now. He started to clamber up the side towards the hatch. He'd never been in a tank before. He reached forward. But before he touched the hatch it sprang open and from inside came a piercing cry:

'HAAAAAALT!'

Fuzzy fell back on to the floor in amazement.

'Who goes there? To the Left Quick March Left Right Left Right Left Left Left! At-ten–shun!'

A small, bristly-haired guinea pig wearing a metal army helmet emerged

from the tank, its little nose twitching.
It looked them up and down with
dark beady eyes.

'Who are you?' asked Coco.

'Er – Private number 19212 – or is it 19121? One or the other. Anyway, it's Private Pat – Pat's short for Patricia, but that's too long to say in a battle situation. *At ease.*' Private Pat pulled herself out of the hatch of the tank and saluted.

'Excuse the commands,' she said, jumping down to the floor, 'but I have orders from the General. No civilians on British Army property. Violation of this order will carry the highest penalties, due to the top-secret special facilities of this particular vehicle. Besides,' she added, prodding Fuzzy's tummy, 'you'd never make it through the hatch.'

'The General?' repeated Coco. 'The general what? General knowledge?'

'Pat is a private,' whispered Fuzzy.

'A private what?' said Coco loudly. 'A private party?'

'This, young lady, is no party,' said Pat soberly. 'This is no party at all.'

'You're right about that,' agreed Coco. 'How long have you been here?'

'Too long,' said Pat sadly, but then she stood straight and proud. 'But a general's gotta do what a general's gotta do.'

'Is he on duty?' asked Fuzzy politely.

'That's an official secret,' said Pat, 'but he went so long ago I've forgotten when he's coming back. How long have I got to put up with you two?'

'We're only here for a week, thank goodness,' Coco said. 'It doesn't look a bit like it did on the website. Except for indoors. How do you get in there?'

'You don't,' said Pat bluntly.

'Well, maybe *you* don't,' boasted

Coco, 'but I will. Just you wait and see.'

'I will wait, and I'll see that you won't.'

'Coco's very good at locks,' said Fuzzy helpfully.

'It's not a question of locks, lady,' said Pat. 'Except the ones on your head. And they're far too short. *Dis–missed*.'

'You can't dismiss me, you know. One used to live with the Queen.'

Pat didn't answer. She turned away and started humming the tune of 'The Grand Old Duke of York'.

She didn't sing the words because she'd forgotten them. She'd also forgotten who the Queen was, but she wasn't going to admit that to Coco.

5
the great escape

When Nigel came out to the garden in the afternoon to feed the guinea pigs, Coco, who was still determined to prove Pat wrong and get into the house, decided to try her hardest to impress him. She cleaned her whiskers and fluffed her rosettes and retied

the bow in her
hair. Then she
sat where Nigel
would notice
her – at the door
to the hutch –
looking lovely.

'Good luck,
Coco,' Fuzzy whispered
as Nigel worked his way around the
bored-looking guinea pigs in the other
hutches.

'She'll need it,' Private Pat snorted.

Nigel's footsteps approached.

He bent down to open the door.

Coco held her breath. Any minute
now, Nigel would realize his mistake
and take her straight to the spa
for a massage. She closed her eyes,
expecting to feel herself being lifted
gently off the ground.

SPLAT!

Something soggy landed on her.
She heard the hutch door clang shut
and the click of a key turning the
latch.

Coco opened her eyes. The world
had gone green.

'I told you,' Private Pat said as
Coco crawled out from under the

slimy lettuce leaf. 'It's only the special guinea pigs who get into the house.'

Coco hardly heard. She'd had enough of Nigel and Private Pat for one day. 'That's *it*,' she said. 'One is going home. Come on, Fuzzy.'

'Going home?' Fuzzy echoed. 'But how can we, Coco? We don't know the way, and even if we find

the house, we can't get in. Ben and
Henrietta are on holiday, remember?'

'I don't care!' said Coco, who
could be a bit silly when she got in a
huff. 'We can stay with Banoffee until
they get back.'

Fuzzy shook his head. 'It's
impossible, Coco. We can't even get
out of this hutch. It's locked.'

Coco frowned. She hadn't thought
of that. If only Eduardo was here
with his satchel full of skeleton keys!
He'd get them out. At the thought
of Eduardo, Coco suddenly felt even
more miserable. She wished she hadn't

been so horrid about his songs — she'd give anything to hear him singing now.

Private Pat spoke up. 'You could escape through the tunnel, I suppose.'

'The what?' Fuzzy and Coco said together. Fuzzy was gazing at Private Pat with new respect, Coco with disbelief at the thought that Pat could have come up with something useful at last.

'The tunnel. I've been working on it since I arrived at the prison camp ten years ago.'

'Don't you mean ten days?' Fuzzy asked.

'Fuzzy's right. Even you can't be that old,' Coco said rudely.

'Probably,' agreed Private Pat cheerfully, ignoring Coco. 'When you've been in prison camp for a long time, you forget things.' She paused and looked at them, puzzled. 'What was I talking about?'

'The tunnel,' Fuzzy reminded her.

'I knew that! The entrance is over here. Under my bed.' Private Pat rummaged about under the hay and then stood back.

Coco and Fuzzy scuttled over to take a look. They found themselves gazing down into a dark hole just wide enough for a guinea pig to squeeze through.

'That's amazing!' Fuzzy said admiringly. 'Just like in the movies!' Fuzzy liked watching TV with Ben. His favourite shows used to be cookery programmes, until that got him into trouble with Scarlet Cleaver. So now he'd started watching action films instead.

'Thanks,' Private Pat said modestly. 'I must say it's been hard work. Moving large quantities of earth with a miniature screwdriver is no picnic.'

'A miniature screwdriver?' Coco repeated. 'Where did you get one of those from?'

'The General gave it to me – to fix the tank, OBVIOUSLY!' It was Private Pat's turn to be rude.

'But what do you do with all the earth?' Fuzzy said hastily before Coco could reply.

'I'm glad you asked me that, soldier,' Private Pat said. She tapped her bottom, then her nose.

'I roll it into pellets and put it in
the toilet tray. Nigel takes it away
thinking it's poo.'

'That's brilliant!' Fuzzy exclaimed.

Coco looked sulky. The truth was,

she felt a bit jealous that Fuzzy was paying Private Pat so much attention when it had been her suggestion to escape in the first place!

'That's not all,' Private Pat said proudly. She sniffed. 'You smell that?'

Fuzzy nodded. 'It's the rotten food, right?'

'WRONG!' Pat cried, tapping her nose, then her bottom again. 'It's poo! I keep the real stuff hidden up the gun barrel of the tank for emergencies. You never know when you'll need ammunition in a place like this.'

'That's disgusting!' Coco said. She

moved to the edge of the tunnel and peered down it. 'Well, what are we waiting for? Let's go.'

'Not so fast, lady!' screeched Pat. 'No one enters the tunnel without a safety helmet.' She scurried over to the tank, scrambled up the side and popped down the hatch. 'Here!' she said, producing two more tin helmets and a miniature screwdriver. She plonked the helmets on Coco and Fuzzy.

'Now can we go?' Coco said, feeling under her helmet for her squished bow.

'Don't be silly. The tunnel isn't finished yet!' Private Pat shouted. 'But you two can help me dig.' Suddenly she grinned. 'Ladies first,' she said, offering Coco the screwdriver.

Four hours later Coco and Fuzzy lay on their backs in the hutch on a thin mat of hay.

'I'm exhausted!' Fuzzy moaned. 'And I've never been so hungry in my life.'

'My nails are ruined!' Coco wailed. 'And my fur is covered in mud.'

'I'm never going on holiday again!' Fuzzy declared.

'And I'm never going to let you go on the computer again!' Coco complained.

'Cut it out, you two,' Private Pat hissed. 'Some of us are trying to sleep.'

'What I don't understand,' Fuzzy said, 'is why we couldn't escape tonight.'

'Yes, why couldn't we?' Coco said crossly. 'We only had five more centimetres to go.'

'We need provisions,' Pat snapped. 'No soldier enters enemy territory unless they're properly prepared. And anyone who approaches that tunnel without orders will be confined to the toilet tray all week. Now GOODNIGHT.' Very soon, Private Pat was snoring softly.

Coco propped herself up on one front paw. 'She's asleep! Come on, Fuzzy, quick!' She got up, shook the

mud out of her fur and scuttled over
to Pat's bed.

Fuzzy heaved himself up. 'What
are you doing, Coco?'

'I'm going to escape of course!'
She pushed Pat gently aside.

'Are you crazy?' Fuzzy hissed.
'What if she wakes up? You don't
want to spend the rest of the week in
the toilet tray, do you?'

'I won't have to,' Coco said,
edging past Pat, who was still snoring.
'By the time Private Poo-Poo finds
out, we'll be long gone.' She jammed
her helmet on and grabbed the

screwdriver. 'Are you coming?'

'I . . .' Fuzzy started. He was going to say he didn't really like leaving Pat after all the trouble she'd taken to help them, but it was too late. Coco had already disappeared into the tunnel. '. . . suppose so,' Fuzzy sighed. There was no arguing with Coco when she was in this mood.

'Pat will be all right,' he told himself. The General would be back to pick her up soon. When she woke up in the morning she might not even remember they had been there! He jumped into the tunnel after Coco and pulled the straw over the hole.

The tunnel was stuffy and narrow, but the guinea pigs were used to it after spending all afternoon digging with Pat. After a few minutes of going downward, the tunnel levelled out before it went up again. Fuzzy could see Coco's furry bottom wriggling along in front of him. He heard scrabbling. Then he felt earth flying through his whiskers. 'Oi! Watch what you're doing, Coco!' he shouted.

Coco didn't hear him. She was too busy digging the last few centimetres of the tunnel. She didn't realize that without removing the soil as Pat had shown them, the freshly dug earth was making the tunnel behind her narrower and more difficult for Fuzzy to squeeze through.

It wasn't long before Fuzzy was stuck.

'I made it!' Coco cried as her nose poked out into cool, refreshing night air. She could smell grass and leaves and trees. She sniffed. Her nose quivered as it identified something familiar. She brushed the soil out of her eyes and looked about. An old

oak tree towered in front of her.
Behind her were swathes of long grass.
Coco gasped. She knew exactly where
she was! The tunnel had come out in
the copse behind their garden!

'Oh . . . oh . . . oh!' Coco
squealed with excitement. Henrietta
and Ben must have driven around
in circles when they got lost on their
way to Furry Towers. No wonder the
house looked like theirs. The horrible
hotel was just around the corner from
where they lived! 'Hurry up, Fuzzy!'
she cried. 'We're in the copse.'

There was no reply.

'Fuzzy?' Coco called. Her brain was buzzing. The copse! It was just a short scuttle across the grass to the hole in the gate and then under the fence to Banoffee's hutch. And of course, the copse was where Eduardo lived. They would see him in the morning. Coco blushed. She hoped he had forgiven her.

Just then the grass behind the tunnel entrance began to move. Coco frowned. It wasn't windy. What could be making it sway like that?

'Fuzzy?' she called again. 'Is that you?'

But it wasn't long before Coco realized it wasn't Fuzzy. Very soon, two yellow lights appeared, like torches. Coco swallowed. She began to tremble. She knew they weren't really torches. She knew from the last time she had been in the copse at night that they were *eyes*. And she also knew whose eyes they were.

A sly face peered out from the tall grass, followed by a red body and long bushy tail.

'Hello,' said the animal, licking its lips.

Coco nearly fainted. She was right. It was Renard the fox.

6
friends reunited

'Aren't you going to tell me what big eyes I've got?' Renard asked.

Coco stood frozen with terror.

'You'd be right. I have got big eyes. They get big when I see something I want to eat.' And he leaned forward and sniffed her, just like Ben sniffed the gravy before he tucked into his Sunday dinner.

'Well, you're not going to eat me!' said Coco bravely, even though her legs were shaking with fear. 'One is not ready to die! There are still things I want to do in this world, like climb up the stairs to the bathroom and use Henrietta's nail brush.'

'A high ambition indeed,' said Renard.

'Yes,' said Coco soberly. 'It is.' She counted up in her head. 'It's twelve steps to the landing and another six to the bathroom.'

'And all I want to do is eat every living thing in this copse, until there is nothing left.'

'That'll take you a while,' said Coco as bravely as she could, 'because the big oak tree's alive and that will take ages to digest.'

'Enough of your cheek!' snapped the fox, and lunged towards her with his mouth open as wide as Coco's when she tried to eat a whole Brussels sprout.

Coco knew if she turned and ran he would catch her. So she did the opposite and forced herself to leap

forward, in between Renard's legs.
Renard stepped backwards in surprise,
trying to butt her with his nose.

Coco looked up. Her whiskers
started to twitch. There
was a rush of air
and a shout. It
was Eduardo,
swinging down
on an old rope
some kids had
tied to the tree.

'*Caramba,
bamba!*' cried
Eduardo as he landed

on the fox's back and grabbed his ears. Renard lifted his head and shook it, trying to throw Eduardo off.

Coco looked up in relief. 'Oh, Eduardo! One is pleased to see you!'

'The pleasure's all one's, señorita. Now run for your life!'

'Quick!' Coco shouted. 'The tunnel!'

'What tunnel?' Eduardo yelled, digging his nails into the fox's fur to stay on.

'This one!' Coco scooted into the mouth of the tunnel.

The fox stopped just short of it. He

shook his head in anger and Eduardo was thrown off. His little body easily plopped into the opening and he crawled after Coco. The fox was left at the entrance, snarling.

'DIG!' said Coco.

Coco and Eduardo dug frantically. It wasn't long before they saw Fuzzy.

'There you are!' Coco exclaimed. 'What have you been doing? Wallpapering the walls?'

'I got a bit stuck,' Fuzzy admitted.

'I told you to hold back on the avocados,' said Coco bossily.

94

'I haven't had any, you silly thing!' Fuzzy said. 'It was the way you tunnelled. You just chucked the loose earth behind you and it made the tunnel narrower.'

'We don't have time to discuss that now,' she said. 'We have to go back to the hotel.'

'But I thought we were escaping?'

'Renard the fox is at the other end. Even Eduardo couldn't stop him.'

'Renard?' Fuzzy repeated in astonishment. 'Eduardo?'

'Yes! The tunnel comes out in the copse!' Coco said impatiently, as if this was the most obvious news in the world. 'I'll explain later.'

'Is Eduardo OK?' asked Fuzzy as he turned round.

'I'm fine.' Eduardo's voice came from behind them.

BOOM!

'*Caramba!* What was that?'

Suddenly it was very dark.

'*Vamos!*' Eduardo shouted. 'The tunnel is collapsing!'

The guinea pigs hurried forward as fast as they could.

'There's definitely no going back to the copse now,' said Fuzzy miserably.

'No. We have to go on,' agreed Coco.

'So I get to go to the hotel after all,' said Eduardo, secretly pleased.

'Yes,' said Coco, 'but don't get your hopes up. It's not going to be much of a holiday.'

7
danger!

By the time the three guinea pigs re-emerged into the hutch in the garden at Furry Towers, it was daybreak.

'Quick! Cover up the tunnel entrance before Pat sees!' Coco ordered.

Who is Pat?' Eduardo asked, smoothing the straw with his toes.

Coco glanced wearily at Private Pat, who was doing sit-ups.

'Ninety-seven . . . ninety-eight . . . ninety-nine . . .' Pat puffed.

'That's Pat,' Coco told Eduardo. 'She's bonkers. Her owner's a general in the army, but the way she carries on anyone would think that she does the fighting, not him!'

'That's not fair, Coco,' Fuzzy said quietly. He turned to Eduardo. 'It was Private Pat who dug most of the tunnel before we even decided to try and escape.' He pointed around the garden. 'As you can see, the hotel isn't exactly what we were expecting.'

Eduardo looked about him and sniffed the air. He took in the rusty hutches and the stinking smell of rotten food. He raised one bushy eyebrow. 'This is the hotel?' he exclaimed. 'What happened to the delicious four-course meals?'

Fuzzy shrugged. 'Search me. We

get squishy old vegetables once a day.'

Eduardo glanced at Coco's muddy fur. 'And the spa, señorita?' he asked gently.

'There is one,' Coco said hastily. She didn't want to admit to Eduardo that she hadn't managed to get into it. 'In the house. I'm going today.'

'But hardly any of the guinea pigs are allowed to go there, Coco,' Fuzzy reminded her.

'Why not?' Eduardo asked.

'Because the five-star treatment is just for the special ones,' Private Pat shouted. 'Not for the likes of those two.' She rolled over and started doing press-ups. 'I told them that yesterday.'

Coco opened her mouth to say something rude, but Eduardo had already scuttled over to talk to Pat.

'You like to keep fit?' he enquired admiringly.

'Yes, I do,' Pat puffed, pushing herself up and down on her scrawny front legs.

'It's very important to train properly when you are a fighter.' Eduardo nodded approvingly. 'Me, I do two hundred push-ups a day.'

'Who are you, anyway?' Pat lifted her head to look at him.

'My name is Eduardo Julio Antonio del Monte.' He bowed.

'Are you a soldier?' she squeaked.

'No.' Eduardo puffed out his chest proudly. 'I am a freedom fighter. I come from far away in the Andean mountains.'

'No way!' Private Pat stood up and started marching on the spot. 'That's where I did my altitude training.'

'Really?' Casually Eduardo dropped his satchel on the ground, reached up and took hold of the tank's gun barrel and started doing chin-ups. 'What a coincidence.'

Suddenly he felt a poke in the ribs. It was Coco with a piece of old celery.

'When one has finished showing off,' she snapped, 'perhaps one would think about how we're going to get out of this hutch!'

'Yes, what are we going to do now the tunnel's collapsed?' Fuzzy said without thinking.

'It's what?' shrieked Pat. 'After all that work with the screwdriver. Who did that?'

'Fuzzy!' Coco said promptly. 'He was too fat.'

'Coco!' Fuzzy answered at the same time. 'She didn't take out the earth properly.'

'I warned you what would happen if you interfered with my tunnel!' Pat yelled. 'It's the toilet tray for you two for the rest of the week or I'll splatter you with poo pellets!'

'What's going on here?' a deep voice said suddenly.

The guinea pigs stopped arguing. They froze. All except Eduardo, who dropped off the gun barrel and started to burrow in the straw.

It was Nigel, the owner of Furry Towers.

'It's breakfast time,' Pat whispered.

Nigel crouched down and pressed

his face against the hutch. He stared intently at the guinea pigs. Coco and Fuzzy glanced at one another. They felt scared. Even though they knew Nigel couldn't understand what they'd been saying (because all humans hear when guinea pigs talk to one another is squeaking and chattering), they didn't know how long he'd been standing watching them.

'Act normal!' Pat ordered, retreating to the toilet tray.

'OK!' Fuzzy began stuffing his face with the bit of celery Coco had used to poke Eduardo with.

Coco pretended to sleep.

But to their horror Nigel didn't go away. Instead he put down the tray of food he'd been carrying, took out his keys and opened the hutch door. The guinea pigs watched his hand creep towards the straw like a giant spider.

'Eduardo!' Coco cried. 'Look out!'

But it was too late. Nigel's hand had closed around Eduardo's back and was pulling him out from under the straw towards the hutch door.

'A silver Agouti!' Nigel closed and locked the door with his spare hand. He stood up and held Eduardo out to examine him. Coco and Fuzzy watched from the hutch. They knew that a silver Agouti was a type of guinea pig – the type that Eduardo was, with black short hair sprinkled with silver and jet black eyes – but they didn't know why Nigel was so interested in him.

'How did you get here?' Nigel sounded puzzled. Then he shrugged.

'Oh well, who cares?' He started stroking Eduardo gently. 'Now you really are special. And you do tricks! I've never seen a guinea pig swinging about like that before.' He tucked Eduardo into his shirt. 'You, my friend, deserve a treat! I'm taking you to the house for a bubble bath.'

The other guinea pigs watched him stride away.

'Right, that's it!' Coco screeched, overcome by jealousy. She scuttled about in fury. 'If Eduardo gets to have a bubble bath, so do I.' She raced over to where Eduardo had dropped his

satchel and pulled out
his skeleton keys.

'What if Nigel
catches you?'
Fuzzy protested.

'I don't care.'
Coco held a thin
key in her delicate
paws and wiggled
it into the lock. The
lock clicked open. 'Anyway, I'm sure
once I'm clean Nigel will see who the
special one is around here,' she said,
sticking her nose in the air, 'and it's
not Eduardo.'

'Wait . . .' Fuzzy had a horrible feeling something was wrong.

Coco wasn't listening. She jumped out of the hutch and scampered across the lawn before Fuzzy could stop her.

Fuzzy thought hard. What could Nigel really want with Eduardo? Why did he care if he did tricks? His mind went back to the newspaper report Coco had been reading the night they found Furry Towers on the Internet. Eduardo was rare, just like some of the stolen guinea pigs. Was there a link? If there was, Eduardo could be in great danger. And now Coco had

dashed off after him. She could be in danger too. He had to do something to save them!

'Pat!' Fuzzy said urgently. He'd had an idea. 'I need to talk to you about the special facilities on the tank.

They don't include communications equipment by any chance, do they?'

Very soon Coco reached the conservatory. She wriggled up the trellis on the outside so she could see if Eduardo was on the counter with the long-haired Sheltie they had seen when they first arrived. (Unlike most guinea pigs, Coco was very good at climbing. She'd learned on the harp when she lived at Buckingham Palace.) When she reached the level of the counter she had to screw up her eyes to see because she was very

slightly short-sighted,
but she could
definitely make
out two guinea
pigs lying on red
velvet cushions
nibbling grapes.

'So much for
not liking hotels,
Eduardo!' Coco
muttered sourly.

Meanwhile, Nigel
was bending over a shallow plastic
bowl full of bubbles, checking the
temperature with his elbow. Coco

closed her eyes and breathed in the scent of blueberries and vanilla. It smelt heavenly.

'Here you go!' Nigel lifted the two guinea pigs gently off the velvet cushions and into the shallow water.

Suddenly a mobile phone rang. Nigel felt in his pockets, then left the room to answer it.

The window was open a few centimetres. Quick as a flash, Coco wriggled in and scurried over to the bath. She tried to climb in but the sides were too slippery – not at all like

the harp strings she had been used to
climbing at the Palace.

'Psst, Eduardo!' she hissed.

Eduardo's face appeared over the
side of the bath. His
whiskers were
covered in
bubbles.
'Señorita!
What can I
do for you?'

'I want to get in, you idiot,' Coco squeaked.

'Good, because I want to get out. I have already done fifty laps.'

Another face appeared beside him. It was the beautiful long-haired Sheltie.

'This is Lulu,' Eduardo said. 'She's a model.' He yawned. 'She knows a lot about shampoo.'

'And facials,' Lulu purred.

'So do I!' Coco felt faint with excitement. She couldn't wait to talk to Lulu. 'Can you climb out, Eduardo?'

'Sure,' he replied. 'I can use this

lilo as a trampoline.' He started bouncing up and down.

'Wait!' screeched Coco. 'I'll make a jump.'

Most guinea pigs can't climb anything much except for a few stairs, which is why they use a jump. Coco balanced a toothbrush on a bar of soap beside the bath. Then she sat on one end of the toothbrush. 'Ready,' she said, squinting up.

'Ready.' Eduardo sprang off the lilo on to the other end of the toothbrush.

There was a splash followed by a

sigh of pleasure as Coco catapulted into the bubbles. 'About shampoo . . .' she began, turning to Lulu.

Eduardo shook himself dry while the girls chattered away about blueberries.

Something was troubling him. It wasn't that he wasn't enjoying himself – he was. In fact he liked holidays a lot better than he had thought he would, though he wasn't going to admit that to Coco. Lying about on a velvet cushion eating grapes made a nice change from fighting the fox and mending his satchel. What he didn't like was the fact that all the other guinea pigs at Furry Towers, especially Fuzzy and Private Pat, didn't get to have treats like him and Lulu.

'All guinea pigs should be equal,'

he muttered, shaking the water out of his ears.

'What was that?' Coco clambered on to the lilo and peered over the side of the bath.

'I said, all guinea pigs should be equal, señorita.'

'Oh, definitely,' Coco agreed. 'Fetch me a towel, would you? I want to keep my ribbon dry.'

'Sure,' Eduardo grumbled, wandering along the counter. 'Anything else?'

'A carrot juice with an umbrella in it would be nice,' came the reply from Coco.

'I was joking!'
Eduardo
shouted back
at her.
Nigel had left the
kitchen door open.
Eduardo could hear
him talking on
his mobile phone
in the hall.

'Yeah, he's definitely a rare breed
. . . a silver Agouti . . . and he does
tricks! He's perfect for your circus.'

Eduardo gasped. Nigel was talking
about *him*!

123

'So you'll pick him up later with the other one . . . the Sheltie?'

And he was talking about Lulu!

'Great. I'll make sure they're ready so you can catch the plane tonight.'

All of a sudden Eduardo realized what was happening. Furry Towers was a fake. Nigel was a crook!

'*Caramba!*' Eduardo whistled. 'So that's why we're special. He's going to sell us to a circus!'

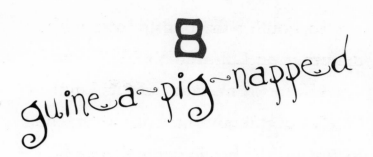

8
guinea-pig-napped

Eduardo rushed back along the counter to the bath. 'Lulu! Coco!' he called. 'It's time to get out. Nigel has terrible plans for Lulu and me!'

'What was that, Eddy?' Lulu called back. 'I can't hear too well. I've got shampoo in my ears!'

125

'Get out of the bath now!' commanded Eduardo.

'Give us a minute,' said Coco. 'We've got conditioner on our fur and it says on the bottle it needs another

ten minutes for that deep-down, all-over, sweet-smelling shine.'

'I don't care if you both smell like a sewer!' shouted Eduardo. 'Get out of the bath! Nigel is going to sell me and Lulu to a circus.'

Coco stood up on the lilo and popped her head over the side of the bath. 'So does that mean I can stay in for a bit?'

'How can you be so selfish and silly at a time like this? The circus owner is on his way! He wants to take us on a plane tonight.'

Coco and Lulu looked alarmed.

'Come on, Lulu, you go first,' said Coco. She wasn't being selfish or silly now.

Lulu looked over the edge of the bath. 'How do I get down?' she asked fearfully.

'Climb down off the lilo,' Coco said, showing her what to do. She held on to the side of the bath with her front paws and swung one back leg over, followed by the other, and dropped down on to the counter.

Lulu copied her.

'Now what?' Coco asked, peering over the edge of the counter. 'It's

too far to jump. And you two can't
climb.'

'But we can fly!' Eduardo grabbed
a shower cap that was lying on the
counter and whipped it up into the air
above his head.

'Excuse me, but where are your
manners?' Coco demanded. 'What
happened to "Ladies first"?'

'It might not be safe, señorita,'
Eduardo explained. 'Especially for
Lulu. I will go first and find something
soft for you to land on.'

Then he took a running jump and
hurled himself off the counter. The

shower cap acted like a parachute and
he floated almost gracefully to the
floor.

'I don't know how
to jump,' said Lulu,
shaking with fear.
'I get carried
everywhere
at home.'

'I'll show you,' said Coco bravely, 'and then you can copy. It's easy, really.'

In truth Coco was pretty scared herself. She'd never jumped down so far. And it would have been easier for her to climb down the trellis outside. But she had to jump to show Lulu it could be done. She looked down at the hard lino floor.

'Hang on,' Eduardo said, and he dashed over to a sponge which was lying not far away on the floor. (It seemed Nigel wasn't a very tidy person.) He pushed the sponge along the floor until it was below the girls.

'There you go,'
he said to Coco.
'Land on
that.'

Coco
shut her
eyes and
jumped.

She felt
herself falling.
She thought she
would never stop. And then she did –
with a bounce, on the sponge.

'Well done,' said Eduardo, taking
her paw so she could leave the sponge

like a high jumper leaving the landing mat.

Coco shook herself. She was still a bit sticky from the conditioner as she hadn't had time to wash it off properly.

'Your turn now, Lulu,' Eduardo said.

They both looked up at Lulu. Lulu looked down at the sponge. She took a deep breath. And then she squealed because a big hairy hand had grabbed her and chucked her into a cage!

'Time to go, rodent. Now, where's your silvery friend?'

It was Nigel. The guinea pigs had been so busy with jumping down from the counter that they hadn't heard him come back in.

Coco dashed for cover. It wasn't too far to the conservatory's curtains. 'I made it!' she gasped.

'Wait for me!' WHOOSH! Eduardo slipped on the wet floor where Coco had shaken herself.

Nigel was stomping around the room. 'Where's that blinking guinea pig?' he muttered. 'Ronald will be here in a minute.' He saw Eduardo struggling to get up. 'Ah, there you are.'

'Come on, Eduardo,' whispered Coco from the curtains. 'Hurry!'

'I can't, señorita! You've made this place as slippery as a Peruvian mud slide!' Eduardo cried.

The doorbell rang.

'Got you just in time.' Nigel grabbed Eduardo and threw him into the cage. 'Ronald doesn't want to hang around. He's flying to the circus with you two tonight.' He put the cage on the counter and went to answer the door.

Coco watched from behind the curtains. She was trembling. What should she do now? What could one little guinea pig do against two big, mean men? She might never see Eduardo and Lulu again. It was unbearable.

Her heart was pounding so loudly in her chest that she didn't hear a strange sound coming from the garden. And even if she had heard it she might not have known what it was. She might even have thought it sounded a little scary. But once the thing that was making the noise came through the door into the conservatory she wasn't scared at all. She was delighted. It was Pat's tank coming to the rescue!

9
battle stations

'Coco! What's going on? We were worried.'

Fuzzy's head popped out of the tank. (He had become so slim after twenty-four hours at Furry Towers that he'd had no trouble slipping through the hatch after Pat.)

'Oh, Fuzzy!' Coco squealed, peeping out from behind the curtains. She had never been so pleased to see her best

friend before. She wanted to hug what was left of him, but there wasn't time for that. 'It's Eduardo!' she shrieked, pointing at the small cage beside the bubble bath. 'And Lulu! Nigel's a crook. He's going to sell them to a circus. We've got to help them, Fuzzy, before it's too late.'

'I thought it might be something like that,' Fuzzy said grimly, 'which is why I came prepared.' He ducked down into the tank and pulled out Eduardo's satchel.

'You brought my keys, Fuzzy!' Eduardo shouted in delight from the cage. '*Caramba*, you're getting smart; like me. Quick. Throw them up. I will help the ladies escape.'

'I'm smart too!' Coco said huffily. 'And I don't need help. You're the one who's in the cage.'

'Thanks to you and your conditioner,' Eduardo growled.

Fuzzy ignored them. He took careful aim and swung the satchel up on to the counter beside the cage door.

Eduardo reached out a paw and grabbed it.

They could hear voices in the hall. Fuzzy lowered his head back inside the tank. 'Pat, quick. Drive behind the curtains.'

'Yes, sir!' Pat's muffled voice came from somewhere inside the tank. She rolled them forward to the shelter of the curtains.

'*Sir?*' Coco exclaimed. 'Why is Pat calling you sir?'

'I had to tell her that Eduardo and I were Special Forces on an undercover operation,' Fuzzy whispered, grinning sheepishly, 'or she'd never have let me use the tank. Now shush.'

A man in a long leather coat with a big hat and bushy beard stepped into the room past Nigel.

'Show me the Agouti,' he said in a deep, rough voice. He took off his hat.

Fuzzy and Coco gasped.

'It's the baddy from the newspaper!' Coco squealed.

'He must have been stealing all the guinea pigs for his circus!' Fuzzy exclaimed.

'What's happening, sir?' Pat's voice floated up from somewhere inside the tank. 'I can't find my compass.'

'We're deep in enemy territory, private,' Fuzzy hissed. 'That's what. Arm the missiles.'

'Right you are, sir.'

There was a funny smell. Coco wrinkled her nose delicately but she was smiling at the same time. 'Pat's poo pellets!' she whispered with glee.

Fuzzy nodded. 'I have a feeling they're about to come in handy.'

Ronald stepped towards the cage, followed by Nigel.

'Let's see the one that does tricks, then,' he said, bending down.

'How's this for a trick, you ugly mug!' Eduardo shouted, swinging the cage door forward with all his might and smacking Ronald in the face with it. 'Ha ha!' he cried as Ronald staggered back into Nigel. 'Come on, Lulu.' He grabbed her paw.

The two of them scampered forward towards the edge of the counter.

'Coco,' Eduardo called, 'the sponge!'

Quick as a flash, Coco scurried across the floor and pushed the sponge into position.

'Go, Lulu!'

This time Lulu jumped without hesitation. She bounced straight off the sponge and behind the curtains, where Fuzzy and Pat were hidden. Fuzzy blushed. Lulu was really very pretty.

'Ready, sir?' Pat's voice came from inside the tank.

'Er, yes!' Fuzzy dragged his attention away from Lulu. He tried to sound brave. 'Let's roll.'

The tank trundled out from behind the curtains.

146

'What's this?' Ronald looked down at his feet in amazement.

'Ready!' Fuzzy shouted, plonking on his tin helmet. 'Aim . . . FIRE!'

POP! POP! POP!

The smell of Pat's poo pellets wafted around the room.

'Don't let them escape!' Ronald roared, hopping about and clutching at his ankles. 'I want them all. I will make millions with this show!'

'Oh no, you won't,' Coco muttered. She was thinking hard. Fuzzy and Pat couldn't hold them off forever with the tank. The poo pellets would run out soon. Even Pat couldn't produce enough poo to defeat two grown men. Suddenly Coco had an idea.

Nigel's face was purple with rage. He didn't look handsome any more. 'I'll get you, you little . . .' He advanced towards Eduardo.

'Too late, loser!' Eduardo threw his

satchel across his shoulders and bent his knees ready to launch himself into the air.

'Wait!' Coco shouted, moving the sponge.

'What do you mean, wait, señorita?' Eduardo shouted back. 'I am about to be exported to a foreign circus to do tricks and you want me to wait? Is this some kind of joke?'

'I've got an idea,' Coco yelled. 'Throw down the conditioner.'

'*Caramba!* Now is no time to think about your hair!' Eduardo scampered about, trying to avoid Nigel, who was grabbing at him with both hands. 'Fuzzy, a little help, please!'

'Coming right up.' The tank changed direction. Fuzzy began firing at Nigel.

'Throw it down!' Coco insisted.

'OK, OK.' Eduardo dashed towards the basin. Luckily the conditioner was just on the edge, where Coco and Lulu had left it. Eduardo pushed.

Coco jumped out of the way as the bottle fell on to the floor beside her.

'Now can I jump?' Eduardo

demanded, running around in circles to avoid Nigel.

'Not yet,' Coco moaned. 'It didn't open.'

'What are you doing, lady? You are crazy!'

'I said, wait!' shrieked Coco. She flipped open the top of the conditioner with her nails. 'OK, now. Jump on the bottle.'

Eduardo didn't stop to ask any more questions. He sailed through the air.

SPLAT!

He landed on the bottle. Pink

conditioner shot out all over the floor.

'We're out of missiles!' Fuzzy yelled.
'Retreat! Retreat!'

Coco and Eduardo jumped on to
the gun barrel and hung on. The tank

trundled back towards the curtains.
The guinea pigs watched, breathless, as
Nigel and Ronald looked round
wildly.

'They're behind the curtains.'
Ronald took a step forward.

'Allow me.' Nigel's face twisted
into a horrible sneer.

'Er . . . shouldn't we be running
away or something?' Lulu suggested.

'No,' Coco said firmly.

'You sure?' Eduardo said
nervously.

'I'm sure. Just wait,' Coco
whispered. 'Any second now . . .'

All five guinea pigs – Eduardo, Fuzzy, Coco, Lulu and Pat, who had got out of the tank – held their breath.

'WHOAOAOAOAO!' Nigel was the first to slip on the conditioner. He slithered to the floor.

'WHOAOAOAOAO!' Ronald slid after him and tripped over Nigel's feet.

'OW!'

'OOOWWWW!'

The two crooks ended up in a tangled, sticky pink mess on the hard tiles, groaning.

Eduardo whistled. '*Caramba*, señorita. You really are the smartest guinea pig I ever met!' He reached out and took her paw.

Coco blushed.

'Yes, jolly good show!' Pat congratulated her. 'I thought you were a complete dimwit, but you've proved me wrong.'

Eduardo rattled his satchel with his free hand. 'Now let's go and free the guinea pigs of Strawberry Park!'

'HOORAY!' they all shouted.

Just then, there was a rumble like thunder. Pat looked up. 'Good heavens!' she squeaked. 'I know that sound. It's the General arriving in the real tank!' She stood to attention.

A second later there was the squeal of brakes.

'Good heavens!' Coco exclaimed. 'I know that sound. It's Ben and Henrietta's car.' She sounded puzzled. 'How come they're here so soon? They're not due back for ages.'

'I sent the General a message,' Fuzzy said proudly, 'asking him to come, and to contact Ben and Henrietta. Pat gave me special permission to use the communications

equipment in the tank. Mind you –'
he looked at the clock – 'I expected it
to take more than twenty minutes for
them all to get here.'

The guinea pigs looked up. A
tall man with big black boots and
a green army jacket was standing
in the conservatory next to Ben and
Henrietta. The three of them were
looking down at Nigel and
Ronald.

'Get me out of here!' Nigel
begged. 'The guinea pigs have gone
crazy. They've attacked.'

'Attacked?' the General repeated.

'Over there!' Ronald's finger shook
as he pointed to the five guinea pigs
lined up beside the curtains. 'They

pelted me with poo pellets from the tank!'

'They escaped from the cage!' Nigel roared.

'They squirted conditioner all over the floor to make us fall over!' Ronald cried.

'Rubbish,' Henrietta said firmly.

'I know who you are,' said Ben, pointing at Ronald. 'I've seen your picture in the paper. You're the one who's been stealing all the guinea pigs.'

'Which means that you . . .' Henrietta concluded, pointing at

Nigel, '. . . are a crook.' She picked up the conditioner and squirted some on Nigel's head. 'Pretending to run a hotel for poor little innocent creatures and selling them off to a circus like that. It's just as well the General called us. Although we were on our way back anyway,' she added in a soft voice, turning to the guinea pigs, 'because we missed you so much and Ben couldn't stop crying.'

'You should be ashamed of yourself,' Ben said as he pulled Ronald's beard. 'I'm going to call the police.'

Henrietta picked her way around the mess, scooped up all five guinea pigs and placed them carefully on velvet cushions with some grapes.

The General stared at Nigel and Ronald. Then he stared at the toy tank. Then he took out his phone and stared at that. Finally he marched over to the guinea pigs. He bent down and tickled Pat under the ears. 'I'm sorry I left you, Private Pat,' he whispered. She squeaked with pleasure. His eyes twinkled as he nodded to each of the guinea pigs in turn. 'Well done, troops,' he muttered so that Ben and Henrietta couldn't hear him. 'I think you could safely say, "Mission accomplished".'

10

home sweet home

It is sometimes said that the best part of a holiday is coming home. And that is certainly what Fuzzy and Coco said about their 'holiday' at Furry Towers. True, they'd made some new friends in Lulu and Pat, and Coco had enjoyed her bubble bath, but they'd also risked losing Eduardo to the circus and they'd all eaten enough soggy celery to last them a lifetime.

Happily, the bad memories were fading now that they were back in Middleton Crescent. They'd had a delicious meal of crisp cabbage and crunchy carrot and were sitting, warm and snug, on their owners' laps. Coco luxuriated as she spread herself out on Henrietta's soft woollen skirt, allowing Henrietta to

stroke her
with her
confident,
reassuring
vet's hands.

Fuzzy was
in his favourite
position: on his back with his legs
in the air, enjoying Ben's tummy
tickling.

'I don't know how she's done this
to herself,' said Henrietta, separating
the new strands of white fur from the
rest of Coco's caramel coat.

Henrietta didn't know that Coco

had rolled in some spilled white paint in Banoffee's garden, in an attempt to make herself look more like Lulu.

'I wonder if it'll come off in the bath, or if I'll have to—'

'Hang on a minute, darling,' Ben interrupted. 'This looks interesting . . .' And he nodded towards the television which was showing the local news.

'Nigel Branston and Ronald Plug have been fined record amounts for running the sub-standard Furry Towers guinea-pig hotel,' said the newsreader, 'and attempting to kidnap rare guinea pigs for the circus. All guinea pigs have now been returned to their owners, including Lulu, the prize-winning white Sheltie.'

'Thank goodness for that,' said Henrietta happily, giving Coco a little cuddle.

'Indeed,' said Ben, cuddling Fuzzy. 'We wouldn't have wanted to lose you two.'

If Ben and Henrietta had been looking, they would have seen Fuzzy wink at Coco. It was a wink that said: they'll never know that we weren't actually special enough to be picked for the circus!

'Just shows you can't believe everything you see on the Internet,' said Henrietta, putting Coco gently down on the floor as she got up to go and have her bath. 'Furry Towers looked wonderful on the website.'

'Lesson learned,' said Ben, as he popped Fuzzy down too and got up to go and make the cocoa. But they both looked back at the television when they heard the next part of the story:

'And finally,' said the newsreader, 'a happy ending for the badly run Furry Towers hotel. It has been bought by a recently retired general, whose guinea pig was a guest at the old hotel. He has promised a complete refurbishment; he'll also be employing a new specialist guinea-pig chef and a top pet beautician.'

'By the way,' Coco said, 'I've been wondering how the General got there so quickly after you sent the message.'

'I wondered that too,' Fuzzy admitted. 'It turned out he was just up the road at a training camp, but he wasn't allowed to take Pat with him. That's why he's taken early retirement – so he doesn't have to leave her on her own again.'

'I'm so glad,' Coco said, 'that he's going to be running the hotel now. I think he understands guinea pigs rather well.'

Fuzzy nodded. 'It was nice of him to give Eduardo the tank to get home in,' he said. 'And Pat was pleased with the new plane he bought her.' He scratched his crest. 'I'd love to get a look at that some time.'

'And I'd love to finally get my blueberry-and-vanilla facial!' Coco giggled. 'You know what, Fuzzy, I think we should go back to Furry Towers and see them after all.'

When Ben and Henrietta were safely in bed Coco popped out into the garden and made her way down to the copse. She wanted to tell Eduardo the good news about Furry Towers, but she also wanted to show him her new white fur, which she hoped made her look a bit more like Lulu. It was drizzling with rain outside, but she didn't let that stop her.

By the time Coco got to the copse she was quite wet. Eduardo was

singing to himself while he tinkered
with the tank.

'I'm Eduardo, the fighter,
Freedom is my choice.
I'll shout and cry for liberty
Until I lose my voice.

In the forests of Peru,
In the copse of Strawberry Park,
I'll fight the fox to save my friends
In daylight and at dark.

I do not look for many thanks
Or gold upon the ground.
For me far greater treasures are
The friends that I have found.'

'That was nice,' Coco said warmly
as Eduardo took a breath. 'I'm glad
you're still writing songs.'

'It's not finished yet,' said Eduardo.
'I think it's fine as it is.'

173

'I don't mean it isn't finished as in it needs more work,' he said. 'I mean it isn't finished because there are two more verses.'

'Oh, I see,' said Coco. 'I'd love to hear them.'

'OK,' said Eduardo, 'they go . . .' and he took a deep breath.

'Before you start . . .' said Coco.

Eduardo let out the breath as a sigh. 'Yes,' he said wearily.

'What do you think of my fur?'

He looked her up and down. She was soaking. She looked like a small, wet otter.

'It's wet,' he said.

She looked down at the ground, disappointed. Then she noticed lots of little white puddles next to her. The paint must have washed out in the rain! No wonder he hadn't noticed the new colour! It wasn't there any more.

'Are you going to finish your song?' Coco asked to change the subject.

'OK,' said Eduardo, and he sang:

'I met the boy named Fuzzy,
He is a real good bloke.
I met the girl called Pat –
She can't take a joke.

I met the lady Lulu
Who likes to look a dish.
But best of all is Coco
My girlfriend she I wish.'

'I'm not sure about the last line,' he said.

'What's wrong with it?' Coco asked.

'I think maybe the words are in the wrong order.'

'It doesn't matter about the wrong order, as long as they are the right words.'

'Yes, they are the right words,' Eduardo said.

'Oh good,' Coco said. 'Can I sing along?'

'With pleasure, señorita.'

And so they sang the song

together, loud and clear, while the
moon rose over the trees and all
the guinea pigs in Strawberry Park
stopped to listen.

the end

You're much better at using
the Internet than Coco is . . .

. . . so why not visit
www.guineapigsonline.co.uk
for lots more fun, giggles and squeaks
with your favourite furry pals!

Quercus

More fur-rific fun with Coco,
Fuzzy and gang in

GUINEA PIGS ONLINE
VIKING VICTORY

A builder is threatening
to bulldoze the copse!
The pals have another
battle on their hands.
With help from Olaf
the guinea pig and
Banoffee's army of guinea
piglets, they are determined to
win the day!

Squeaking in a shop near you from
Summer 2013

Quercus